THE MYSTERIOUS TALE OF
GENTLE JACK
— AND —
LORD BUMBLEBEE

Translation by
GELA JACOBSON

Dial Books
NEW YORK

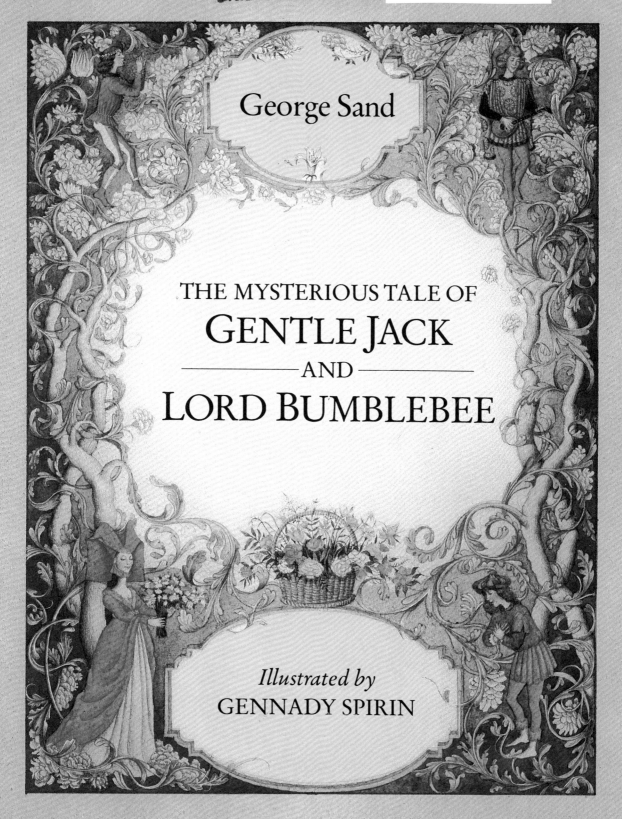

George Sand

THE MYSTERIOUS TALE OF
GENTLE JACK
— AND —
LORD BUMBLEBEE

Illustrated by
GENNADY SPIRIN

George Sand

1804–1876

Amandine Lucile Aurore Dupin, who called herself George Sand, was born in France in 1804. Her father died when she was small, and her mother left her with her grandmother at Nohant, a country estate. She married and had a daughter and a son, but the marriage eventually ended in divorce and she moved to Paris with her children. There she began her writing career and adopted the pseudonym she used for the rest of her life.

Supporting herself and her children chiefly by her writing, George Sand wrote some eighty novels, as well as many plays, stories, and essays. Her work enjoyed great popularity and was based on her love of nature and her belief in social change. She lived an unconventional life for her times and held views that were considered radical – among them, that women should have the same freedoms as men. She wore men's clothes as a sign of her defiance of social custom.

During the time of revolution in France in 1848 George Sand started her own newspaper. Later she left Paris and returned to Nohant, having enjoyed the company of many of the era's well-known writers and artists, including the composer Frédéric Chopin, with whom she lived for a time. Among her last published work was *Tales of a Grandmother*, a collection of Breton fairy tales that she told to her own grandchildren. George Sand died in 1876.

PART
ONE

How Gentle Jack
Met Lord Bumblebee but Could
Not Stay with Him

Once there was a man and wife who had seven children. Three were girls and four were boys, the youngest of whom was known as Gentle Jack.

The man's name was Mr. Stammerer, and he was gamekeeper to the king of the country. He had a handsome house right in the middle of the forest, with a garden in a little clearing beside a stream that wound its way through the wood. But the gamekeeper was a wicked man and didn't consider himself wealthy enough, so he would cheat and rob those who journeyed through the forest, and secretly sell the king's game. But if he caught a poor man taking even three tiny sticks of dead wood for his fire, he would throw him into prison. If a rich person bribed him well, though, Mr. Stammerer would let the man hunt in the royal forests to his heart's content.

Mrs. Stammerer wasn't quite as wicked as her husband, though she, too, was very fond of money.

The couple's six oldest children, who had been brought up to steal and lie like their parents, were thoroughly bad. Their parents loved them very much though. Gentle Jack was the only one they ill-treated because, they said, he was too stupid and too timid to follow the others' example.

When his brothers and sisters saw that their parents hated Jack, they began to taunt him and make fun of him. He bore their teasing patiently, but it made him very sad, and he would often go off alone into the forest to cry and to pray that his parents might love him as much as he loved them.

Now, in this forest there was an old, hollow oak tree that Jack was particularly fond of because it was remote and difficult to find among the rocks and bramble patches that surrounded it.

One day Jack, who had been more ill-treated than usual and was feeling especially sad, was lying sobbing at the foot of the tree, when he felt something sting him on the arm. He looked up and saw a huge bumblebee, which sat there without moving and stared at him in a most insolent fashion.

Jack took hold of the bee by its wings and gently placed it on the palm of his hand.

"Why did you hurt me, when I have done nothing to hurt you?" he asked. "Go on, fly away and be happy."

Then Jack, who wasn't such a simpleton that he didn't know all about the healing properties of the forest herbs, picked a big bunch of their leaves and made a pad of them. After washing his painful arm in the stream, he laid the pad on it and fell fast asleep.

When he awoke, he was astonished to see a tall, fat gentleman dressed in black from head to toe, standing in front of him. The gentleman stared at Jack with enormous round eyes and said in a loud booming voice, "You have done me a service I shall never forget. Come, child, ask for whatever you most desire."

"Alas, Sir," replied Jack, shaking with fright. "My parents don't love me, and I do so wish that they would."

"That is a very difficult wish to grant," replied the gentleman in black. "But still, I will do what I can for you. You are kind but you need to become clever."

"Oh, Sir!" exclaimed Jack. "If, in order to become clever, I must also become wicked, then please don't make me clever. I would far rather remain stupid and continue to be kind."

"And what do you expect to achieve by being kind in a world

full of wicked people?" asked the gentleman.

"Alas, Sir, I don't know how to answer your question," said Jack, who was becoming more and more frightened. "I'm not clever enough for that. But I have never done anyone any harm. Please don't make me want to, or give me the means of doing so."

"You are a fool!" exclaimed the gentleman. "I don't have time to persuade you to change your mind now; but we will meet again, and if you have anything to ask of me, remember that I can refuse you nothing."

"You are very kind, Sir," replied Jack, whose teeth had begun to chatter with fear.

The gentleman turned round, the sunlight caught his great black velvet cloak, showing it first to be a deep blue and then a magnificent violet. His beard began to bristle and his cloak started to swell. He let out a muffled roar more terrifying than that of a lion and, taking off clumsily, he flew away through the branches of the oak tree and disappeared from view.

Jack rubbed his eyes and wondered whether he had been dreaming. Then he picked up his stick and started for home, afraid he would be beaten again for having stayed out so long.

He had hardly set foot in the house when his mother said, "Ah, so there you are. Here is the fool who isn't even aware of his good luck!"

After she had scolded him, she told him that a Lord Bumblebee had been in the forest and that he had stopped at the gamekeeper's house. He had eaten an enormous jar of honey, which he paid for with a real gold coin and, having examined all the children one after the other, had said to Mrs. Stammerer, "Now then, Madam, do you not have a younger child?"

Having learned that there was a seventh child who was only

twelve years old and who was known as Gentle Jack, he had exclaimed, "Oh! What a beautiful name! That's the very child I'm looking for. Send him to me. I will make his fortune." Upon which he had walked out of the house without another word.

"But," said Jack in astonishment, "who is this Lord Bumblebee? I've never met him."

"Lord Bumblebee," replied his mother, "is a rich nobleman who has just arrived in this country. He is going to buy a vast estate and a beautiful castle near here. He seems to have taken a liking to your name, so you must go and see him at once. I'm sure he wants to give you a magnificent present."

"And where will I find him?" asked Jack.

"You really must be very stupid if you don't know where to find a man everybody knows. Go on, hurry, and make sure you bring whatever he gives you straight back here. Otherwise there'll be trouble!"

As Jack was walking in the direction of the castle his mother had pointed out to him, he began to feel tired and faint from hunger. He sat down under a fig tree to rest, when he heard a swarm of bees buzzing above his head. Standing on tiptoe he could just reach a beautiful honeycomb in a hollow in the tree. He thanked heaven and ate a little of the honey. He was about to go on his way again when, from the hollow in the tree, a piercing voice cried, "Seize that wicked child! That thief has been stealing our riches! Tear him to pieces!"

Poor Jack was scared half to death!

"Alas, my lady honeybees," he begged, "forgive me. I was dying of hunger and you have such riches. Truly, I thought at first that it was gold, and it was only when I tasted it that I found it was something more precious than even the finest gold."

"He's not so stupid after all," said a soft, gentle voice. "And for his pretty compliments, I pray you, dear Majesty, my mother, to pardon him and let him continue on his way."

The queen bee decided to be merciful, and Jack was allowed to leave unharmed; but as he looked back, he beheld the most beautiful sight. The fig tree with the honeycomb was surrounded by a fine mist, bathed in a golden light. In this haze he could see hundreds of delicate creatures dancing and flying around one another. They were maidens in golden robes, holding hands and flying in a merry dance, as light as thistledown, around the crown of the tree. The sound of their buzzing and humming was like joyful music. At last, however, the sun sank behind the trees so that Jack was unable to see them any more. And so he turned around again and went on to Lord Bumblebee's castle.

He had walked for a long time and was about to drop with fatigue, when he saw a bright light through the trees.

He turned his footsteps to face it and found himself in front of an enormous castle whose walls, towers, and spires rose up like great cliffs above him.

Surely, this must be the castle of some great king, thought Jack. He walked around it and was amazed to see that it looked both magnificent and threatening at the same time. Hesitantly, he crossed an arched bridge and, taking his courage in both hands, knocked on the huge door. The gatekeeper said, "If you are Gentle Jack, come in. We have been expecting you."

He was given a meal and was surprised to find that all the dishes were made out of clear, sweet honey. He would have preferred a piece of bread and some hot soup, but he didn't dare ask for them. Later, he was shown to a bedchamber. The sound of music and the clattering of saucepans from the kitchen made sleep

impossible, so he decided to explore the castle.

The first room he came to was a vast gallery lined with columns, in which a great ball was being held. Jack watched noblemen dressed in black velvet with gold braid leading their ladies to the dance. It was a truly splendid sight!

The older gentlemen sat at a long table laden with delicious food. The musicians in the balcony were blowing their trombones and trumpets with all their might. Jack watched for a long time. The feast was magnificent. The guests had everything anyone could possibly desire, and yet they didn't seem to be enjoying themselves. The dancers were stiff and unbending and looked around with haughty expressions. People weren't talking to one another, and nobody smiled. No one seemed to notice Jack, and he felt very lonely.

I think I'll go to the kitchen. Perhaps the people there are in a better mood, he decided. But he walked in just as the cook was boxing the kitchen boy's ears and a servant was pocketing half a dozen silver spoons. Here, too, everyone was in a bad temper, so Jack walked on until he found himself in a room where black-clothed gentlemen and overdressed ladies with sullen faces were sitting around a green baize table, playing a game of dice with enormous nuggets of gold. None of them looked at the others; each stared only at the rolling, golden dice, and Jack fled quickly to another room. There he saw guests who were greedily devouring the delicate foods and behaving not at all as decent people should.

Jack let himself be carried along by the crowd. There was a lot of pushing and shoving, but nobody stopped to apologize. Soon he found himself back in the ballroom once again. But now it was all very different. Everyone was chattering loudly, and those who had been drinking wine were bawling stupid songs at the top of their voices. Jack thought, At first sight it seemed as if here was a group of happy, good people, but now I can see only black looks around me. If anyone laughs, it is only out of malice.

At last the feast came to an end. It seemed to Jack as if the people all turned into bumblebees and flew away through the windows. He rubbed his eyes and wondered if he was awake or dreaming. Then he slipped into the park and found a quiet spot to sleep under a tall tree.

When he awoke, quite refreshed, he saw a tall, fat gentleman standing in front of him. He was dressed from head to toe in clothes of velvety black and looked so like the gentleman Jack had seen in his dream beneath the oak tree that he thought they must be one and the same.

"Jack," said the nobleman, "you did well to come and see me, as I wish to do you a good turn."

"Is it really because my name is Gentle Jack?" the boy asked timidly.

"Yes, it really is because your name is Gentle Jack," replied Lord Bumblebee. "You may choose what you want."

Jack was embarrassed. He didn't want any of the things he had seen in the castle. They all seemed to him to be too beautiful and too costly for him to ask for any of them. When he had thought for a bit, he said, "If you could make my parents love me, I would be most obliged to you."

"First tell me why your parents don't love you," said Lord Bumblebee. "You seem to me to be a very nice boy."

"Alas, Sir," replied Jack. "They always tell me it's because I'm too stupid."

"So," said Lord Bumblebee, "we must make you clever."

"And what must I do in order to become clever?"

"You must learn sciences, my young friend. I possess many skills, and I can teach you magic and witchcraft. But, in order to learn them, you will have to come and live with me and be my son."

"You are most kind, Sir," said Jack, "but I have parents already, and although they have other children they love more than me, they might need me some day and it would be wrong of me to leave them."

"As you wish," said Lord Bumblebee. "I'm not forcing you. Good-bye, my dear Jack. If you should change your mind, or if you want something else, come and see me. You will always be welcome."

Upon which Lord Bumblebee vanished into a rosehedge, and Jack found himself all alone.

When he returned home and saw his father's house in the distance, he felt happy and said to himself, "Without knowing it, Lord Bumblebee has given me the means to make my parents love me. Once I tell them I refused to accept any other parents, they will see that I'm not a bad-hearted boy."

Mrs. Stammerer was waiting for him impatiently at the bottom of the orchard. He began to run toward her intending to throw himself into her arms, but she pushed him away and asked, "Well, what have you brought back? Where is the present he gave you?"

And when his parents discovered that he had brought back nothing, and that he hadn't wanted to become the heir of a man who was richer than the king himself, they began to beat him.

Jack, in tears, begged his parents to tell him what he must do to please them, promising that if they really wanted him to go and live with Lord Bumblebee, then he would do so.

His parents then dressed him in rags and sent him back to Lord Bumblebee, hoping to make him believe that they couldn't afford to clothe the boy. And they ordered Jack to ask for a large sum of money.

Jack was dreadfully ashamed to appear before Lord Bumblebee dressed like a beggar. However, he was well received by the lord, who seemed to be a kind man and to be fond of Jack, although Jack couldn't understand why.

"Jack," he said, "I am not displeased to see that you are able to think of yourself. Take whatever you wish."

Then he led Jack down a winding stone staircase until they stood at last in front of a heavy, iron-clad door. The gentleman pulled a huge key out of his pocket and unlocked the door, which opened with a loud creak. Lord Bumblebee raised his lantern. "Ah! Oh!" Jack was speechless with amazement. He found himself in a room full of glittering, glistening silver and gold and precious stones. On cloths of red velvet stood intricately engraved jugs and bowls, overflowing with strings of pearls and diadems. There were fiery red rubies, brilliant blue sapphires, and shimmering white, mysterious opals. The floor was so thickly carpeted with gold ducats that it was impossible not to walk on them.

"Take whatever you wish," repeated Lord Bumblebee, adding scornfully, "so that your parents don't die of hunger!"

Jack did as he was told. He filled his pockets with the gold coins, and though he would have liked to have taken some of the jewels, he said to himself, "Father would certainly not be pleased if I took these bits of glass home to him. He's forever talking about gold ducats." The innocent lad didn't realize that the stones were worth more than all the gold coins put together. Then he thanked Lord Bumblebee politely. He felt like calling him "Your Majesty" because so rich a man could only be a king. The homeward journey seemed endless to him, for the gold weighed very heavily in his pockets, so he stopped for a rest under his oak tree.

Meanwhile, his brothers and sisters who had come to meet him, with the intention of robbing him, found him under the tree. They fell on him shouting, "Give us the gold!" Gentle Jack pleaded, "Let me take the gold home, so that father can see that I did everything he ordered me to do. Then you can have it!" But they took no notice of him, emptied his pockets, and filled their own.

Immediately, a thunderous roaring was heard in the oak tree and a huge swarm of bumblebees dived at Jack's brothers and sisters, stinging them unmercifully. They dropped the gold and fled.

Jack gathered up all the gold and returned home.

Mr. Stammerer, who was only interested in the money, greeted him warmly for once and merely scolded him for being a lazy-bones and a weakling who didn't have the strength to carry twice as much.

But, next day, when Mr. Stammerer went to count the gold with his wife, he was amazed to see it melt in his fingers and spread across the table as a yellow, sticky liquid which turned out to be honey — and bad, bitter-tasting honey at that.

"Truly, Lord Bumblebee must be a great sorcerer," said Mrs. Stammerer, angrily washing her table. "Instead of asking him for money, we should send him a present."

"Of course," replied Mr. Stammerer. "Let us send him the best honey from our hives. I think he would pay us well for that."

The next day they tied a barrel of superb honey onto the back of a donkey and sent Jack off to Lord Bumblebee.

But no sooner had he reached the fig tree where he had seen and heard such surprising things, than a huge swarm of honeybees flew out of the tree and fell upon the donkey, which galloped off, leaving the barrel on the ground.

Then there appeared in front of Jack two beautiful ladies, escorted by a brilliant company of courtiers.

"Child," said the elder of the two, who was the queen, "leave that miserable barrel of honey that you were taking to the king of the bumblebees and take him this message, which will please him far more. Tell him that the queen of the honeybees is tired of war, that she knows the hornets and bumblebees are now too numerous and too powerful to be defeated in pitched battle. Tell him I will give him my daughter's hand in marriage, on condition that he leave our hives in peace and that he will be content with a large part of our treasure, which my daughter will bring as her dowry."

Having said this the queen disappeared, along with her daughter and all the court.

Jack went and told Lord Bumblebee how his parents had given him a barrel of beautiful honey, how the queen of the honeybees had taken it from him and had instead given him a message for the king of the bumblebees.

"As you are very wise," added Jack, "perhaps you could tell me where I might find this king — unless you are he, which is what I believe!"

"That's all just dreams and fantasies," laughed Lord Bumblebee. "Very well, very well, Jack, you have delivered your message. Now let us talk about you, my boy. You see that you will

never be able to do right in your parents' eyes. Would you like to stay with me? You will never have anything to fear from them again, and you will become such a clever man that you will rule the whole world."

Jack sighed and didn't answer. Upon which Lord Bumblebee turned his back on him.

Then Jack became dreadfully afraid without knowing why. He returned home and told his parents all that had happened. Mr. Stammerer scratched his head and said to his wife, "There's magic in all this, you know!"

Turning to Jack, he said, "Child, go back at once to Lord Bumblebee. Tell him that your father gives you to him and take care not to show any signs of distress."

So Jack, with a heavy heart, left for Lord Bumblebee's castle.

Lord Bumblebee received Jack most warmly. He dressed him in magnificent clothes, gave him a beautiful bedchamber, had him eat at his own table, and engaged three pages to wait on him. Then he began to instruct Jack in the art of magic.

Not so long after an extremely beautiful and wealthy princess arrived in the country accompanied by a great queen, who was her mother, and who had come to arrange a marriage between the princess and Lord Bumblebee. The business was soon settled, and after Lord Bumblebee was married, he seemed to be twice as wealthy as before.

His wife was very pretty and very lively, and she treated Jack in a most friendly manner, but he found himself unable to love her. She had the same over-fondness for eating honey and syrup as Lord Bumblebee, which Jack found so unpleasant. On top of that she was miserly and made everyone work very hard indeed. The poor people remained very poor because it appeared that to earn money they had to be either very learned, very strong, or very skillful. And soon it was clear that the people were becoming very wicked — some because they were too well-off, others because they weren't well-off enough. They began to quarrel and to hate each other. Parents reproached their children for not growing up fast enough to earn money; children reproached their parents for not dying soon enough to leave everything to them. Husbands and wives stopped loving each other because Lord and Lady Bumblebee, who set the example, couldn't stand one another. Having married for money, they constantly taunted each other about their backgrounds: Lady Bumblebee mocking her husband for being a mere commoner, and Lord Bumblebee scornfully calling his wife a silly little goose obsessed with nobility. Sometimes they would even hurl coarse insults at each other, with His Lordship accusing Her Ladyship of being miserly, and Her Ladyship branding His Lordship a thief.

Finally, when Jack was fifteen years old, Lord Bumblebee took him by the arm and said, "My young friend, you will be my heir since the fates have decreed that I shall have no children from my marriage. So you will be very rich; indeed, you already are, as everything I have belongs to you. But, when I am gone, you will have to fight many battles in order to hold onto your wealth, because my wife's family hates me. The bees are plotting against me and are only waiting for the right moment to fall upon my lands and take everything they claim belongs to them.

"Therefore, it is time for me to teach you my secrets so that cunning can save you from force when I am no longer with you. Come with me."

Upon which Lord Bumblebee took Gentle Jack in his carriage

to the oak tree where he and Jack had first met. When they arrived, Lord Bumblebee dismissed the coachman and, taking Jack by the hand, sat the boy down among the roots of the tree.

"Taste these acorns," he said to him. "They are good."

Jack ate them with pleasure. Instantly he was overcome by drowsiness, and it seemed to him that he could only see and hear Lord Bumblebee as if in a dream.

First Lord Bumblebee appeared to knock on the bark of the tree. The tree opened and inside Jack saw a beehive with pale golden honeycombs — each with a bee shut away securely in a tasty, clean cell.

Then Lord Bumblebee began to buzz, and climbed up the tree, beating with his wing and his leg on the door of the queen's cell. She hastily drew the bolts and barricaded herself inside. Lord Bumblebee let out a great roar like the sound of a hunting horn, and thousands . . . millions . . . billions of bumblebees, hornets, and wasps began to appear, at first like a distant cloud, and then like a terrible army which hurled itself at the hive. The bees came out to defend themselves, and Jack found himself watching a furious battle in which each combatant tried to pierce an enemy with its stinger or to bite off its head. The fighting became even more horrible when, from the branches of the tree, an army of ants descended, who, instead of taking sides in the conflict, seemed intent only on killing at random so as to carry off and eat the corpses. Each time a wounded insect fell, twenty ants grabbed it with their pincers, bit it, pulled it this way and that, and when they had killed it, they called twenty more of their companions to carry the body to their anthill. In all the confusion the honey, running out through the broken doors of the cells, held both combatants and thieves alike so fast that a great number died from suffocation, drowning, or from being pierced through by their enemies. At last the hornets remained masters of the battlefield, and soon a repulsive orgy was under way. The victors, stuffing themselves with honey and trampling over the corpses of innocent victims, became so bloated that many of them collapsed and rolled into a great heap with the dead and dying.

As for Lord Bumblebee, who had been presented with the keys to the hive on a silver platter, he began to laugh in an evil fashion and, grabbing Jack by the scruff of his neck, he cried, "Go on then, coward, take your share of the spoils, because all this killing has been for your benefit. Go on, take advantage of it! Eat, plunder, loot, kill!"

And he hurled Jack into the depths of the hive. Poor Jack struggled to escape and, rolling down the tree trunk, fell into the anthill, where he was instantly seized by thirty million pairs of pincers which tore at him so horribly that he gave a great cry and woke. When he opened his eyes, he saw that everything was exactly as it had been when he had fallen asleep: The oak tree was closed, the anthill had disappeared, and Lord Bumblebee was his usual calm self and was looking at Jack with a mocking smile.

"Well, Master Sleepyhead," he said to him. "Is this the way you attend to your first lesson? Must you fall asleep when I am trying to explain the laws of nature to you?"

"I beg your pardon," replied Jack, who was still horror-struck at what he had witnessed. "I had a terrible dream. I seem to remember that you were telling me to kill, plunder, and eat."

"Something like that," said Lord Bumblebee. "I was explaining the natural history of hornets and bees to you. The bees work for a purpose; they are very skillful, very industrious, very rich, and very miserly. The hornets are not such good workers and don't

know how to make honey, but they have a great talent — they know how to take. So you see that, in this world, you must rob or be robbed, murder or be murdered, be a tyrant or a slave. It is up to you to choose: Do you wish to conserve wealth like the bees, amass it like the ants, or steal it like the hornets? The surest way, I believe, is to let others do the work and then take from them. Take, take, my boy, by force or by cunning; it's the only way to achieve happiness. There, my friend, I've said my last word on the subject. Choose, and if you wish to be a bumblebee, I will have you admitted as a magician like me."

"And what must I do to become a magician?"

"Take an oath to abandon compassion and that virtue which men call honesty."

"Do all magicians swear to this oath?" asked Jack.

"There are those," replied Lord Bumblebee, "who swear to exactly the opposite and who make it their business to serve, protect, and love all living creatures. But they are just fools."

"Well, Lord Bumblebee," replied Jack, "you haven't succeeded in making me clever, because I prefer those spirits to yours, and I have no desire whatsoever to learn how to plunder and to kill. I thank you for your good intentions, but I request your permission to return home to my parents."

"Fool," replied Lord Bumblebee. "Your parents are hornets who have forgotten their origins."

"Well, then," replied Jack, "I will go into the wilderness and join the good spirits."

"No, my young friend, you will not," said Lord Bumblebee in a terrible voice, rolling his huge eyes like two blazing coals. "I will sting you to death!"

So saying, Lord Bumblebee stretched his wings and once more

took the shape of a hideous insect. He set off in furious pursuit of Jack, who ran as fast as his legs could carry him. For a time Jack managed to beat him off with his hat, but finally, when he saw that he was losing ground, he leaped headlong into the brook. He swam quickly downstream, but the bumblebee kept flying at his eyes trying to blind him so that he was forced to risk suffocation by swimming under water. Then Jack, knowing that he was close to death, cried, "Help me, good spirits!"

In a flash a dragonfly with blue wings appeared out of a clump of wild irises and flew alongside Jack.

"Follow me," she told him. "Don't be afraid."

She flew in front of him and, all at once, a heavy downpour began, stopping Lord Bumblebee in his tracks.

PART
TWO

How Gentle Jack
Reached the Enchanted Island at Last
and Why He Could Not Stay There

Gentle Jack swam and swam, and the stream became a river and the river a broad estuary, and when he grew tired, he felt himself being carried along by the current without having to move an arm or a leg. He fell asleep, and when he awoke, he found that the current had carried him far out to sea. "What kind of water is this," he asked himself, "that doesn't let me drown?"

Fear returned at finding himself so alone in the sea. But then he caught sight of an eagle in the sky carrying an oak twig. So land can't be too far away, he thought. And soon he saw an island, whose cliffs rose steeply from the sea. His spirits revived and he swam strongly toward it.

Nimbly Jack climbed the cliffs and was amazed that everything seemed so easy to him.

He found himself in a warm meadow full of sweet-smelling flowers and herbs. A beautiful white narcissus bent over, brushed, and kissed him gently on the cheek, saying, "Here you are at last, dear Jack. We have been waiting for you." The daisies laughed merrily and whispered to each other, "What a jolly time we'll have now that Jack is here."

"Patience," replied the narcissus. "We must first wait for our queen." She invited Jack to rest for a while in the grass and offered him a soft pillow of fragrant herbs. As Jack fell asleep, the delicate perfume of the balm wafted over him, the lilies of the valley told him a good-night story, and the wild violet played him a sweet melody.

At last he was woken by the sound of happy voices. All around him the flowers were singing and dancing, the quaking-grass was beating time on its castanets, and the linden trees were swinging their blossoms to and fro like tiny bells.

"Thoughtless children," Jack heard a soft voice say. "Don't you have some good news for me this morning?"

At once a thousand voices cried, "Gentle Jack is here! Gentle Jack is here!" And, as if a curtain were being drawn aside, the plants parted and revealed to Jack's charmed eyes the gentle face of their queen. She was the meadowsweet, that beautiful, elegant, slender, perfumed flower that grows in the spring and loves cool and shady places.

"Get up, my dear child," she said to Jack. "Come and kiss your godmother. I've known you since the day you were born and have waited for you for so long."

Joyfully he kissed her hand, and she took him in her arms. Then she smiled at the meadow plants, and it was as if this smile touched all the flowers, grasses and herbs like a magic wand and turned them into fairies and nymphs.

All of a sudden the meadow was full of people. Jack could hardly believe his eyes. There were children, as sweet as cherubs, who chased each other and turned somersaults, and lovely maidens who sat plaiting flowers into each other's hair. Young folk made music and danced while old folk sat and watched.

The queen took Jack by the hand and introduced him to her subjects as her dear guest. Everyone greeted him with great affection.

Then she said, "Go, you're free to do whatever you want. Enjoy yourself and be happy, because you can only stay here for a hundred years. Open your eyes wide and learn from us!"

"Good Queen," replied Jack, "I'm most willing to learn; I've wasted so much time already. But who will teach me?"

The fairy smiled. "Everyone, Jack, everyone. My children know as much as I do, because I shared my knowledge with them thousands of years ago. As true good spirits, they are eager to show you whatever you wish to know. And bear in mind," she went on, "that when your time in this fairy kingdom is at an end, I shall call you to me and talk to you about your past and your future."

"Oh, godmother," cried Jack in terror, "surely you won't leave me? Not now, when for the first time in my life I know what it is to have a mother."

"Never fear, Gentle Jack," assured the fairy. "I will remain among you, and you may come to me whenever you wish."

Then Jack was comforted and, with a glad cry, he rushed to join the happy crowds. Jack was delighted to find a feast set out. He hadn't eaten for a very long time. There was a nourishing soup, exactly as he liked it, then a dish of corn and nuts and vegetables, which he had never tasted before. The wine, served in bluebell glasses, was made from the nectar of flowers, and for dessert there were so many strange fruits that Jack couldn't try them all.

Then the dancing began. Musicians took up position all around. They blew on their pipes, scraped on their fiddles, and plucked at their lutes with great skill. The grasses made heavenly music on their sweet-sounding violins. They were lifted up into the air by the spring breeze and played there so merrily that their melodies set the feet of the nymphs and fairies tapping and they all joined hands in a round dance. Then they began to dance more difficult figures — eights and spirals which they unraveled again with apparent ease. Jack was drawn into the center of the circle by two field violets and found that he, who had never danced before, was able to follow all the steps and to dance along with the others as if he had been doing it all his life.

Then a couple — the huge ground ivy and the tiny daisy — detached themselves from the others and danced a magnificent *pas de deux*. The ivy tossed the graceful maiden high into the air and caught her again, and then the two of them whirled round in a circle, so that Jack felt dizzy just watching them.

Everyone living in this fairyland knew that no harm could befall him. No accident ever had unpleasant consequences. On one occasion some youngsters climbed the cliffs to test their strength. Suddenly, a huge rock broke away from the cliff face and fell into a group of older fairies, who were so deep in conversation that they had forgotten everything around them. Several of them were injured and cried out in pain. Immediately, the other fairies rushed to comfort them. They directed the force of their good thoughts and wishes onto the injured, and when the queen appeared her smile healed the wounds.

Jack got to know a young great burnet. The boy attracted him with his curly red hair and his big black eyes, and they became fast friends. "Just call me Burnie," said the burnet. "That's my nickname."

Together they began to explore the island. They discovered a beautiful grotto from where they could watch the waves rushing in from the sea.

The burnet showed his new friend all kinds of animals. He knew all the creatures that lived in the damp darkness of the caves, and he could talk to the birds as if he were one of them.

Once there was a thunderstorm, and the lightning shot down to earth in blazing zigzags like a heavenly firework display. The thunder rumbled and rolled, and when it was all over, it seemed to Jack as if he had been watching the most wonderful play.

As Jack lay there on his back looking up into the sky, he caught sight of an eagle which was circling high in the air above them. "He's watching over our island with his sharp eyes," explained Burnie. "You see, the birds are our best friends."

When evening came, Jack rejoined the other fairies. It was almost dinner time. As all were skilled in the art of cooking, they prepared the dishes together. Jack looked on inquisitively, and his mouth began to water. There were golden yellow millet soufflés, crunchy buckwheat pancakes, mushrooms, and of course, the foaming nectar wine.

The day drew slowly to a close. The old goatsbeard lit the glowworm and began to puff on his pipe, which he had filled with dried flower stamens. The dandelion boys and forget-me-not girls clustered round him and he began to tell his fantastic fairy stories. As he talked, more and more children came and sat down quietly around him, and even the meadow cranesbill forgot to rattle. Soon the little children fell asleep and were gently covered with cotton-grass blankets. Then night fell. The moon climbed slowly and majestically over the sea and bathed the island in its silvery light. The wind whispered in the trees, and the flower fairies strolled along the gentle paths that led either down to the water or up into the hills.

The moon had long since set and the stars gone out, when Jack fell peacefully asleep on a soft pillow of moss. He woke up to a bright morning, and the queen stood before him.

"Good morning, Jack," she said. "Get up and come with me!" She led her godson to the top of the highest peak on the island, from which the beauties of her kingdom could best be admired.

Then she began to speak and her voice was sad. "My dear child, the hundred years of which I spoke are now past."

"A hundred years?" Jack stared at the beautiful fairy in disbelief. "But it was only yesterday that I arrived on your island!"

"That's right, my child. In the land of men a hundred years have passed since you fled. Here on my island, a hundred years seem like just a single day."

"Must I leave the island, godmother?" he asked anxiously. "Please don't desert me, don't send me away. I can't live anywhere but here, and I'll die of grief if I'm parted from you."

"I will never forsake you, Jack," replied the queen. "And you may stay with us if you wish, but listen to what I have to tell you, and then you will see what you must do.

"The land where you were born is called the Kingdom of the Bumblebees, and Lord Bumblebee has been crowned as its king. Before your birth it was a land like any other, a mixture of goodness and evil, of good and bad people. I happened to be passing at the very moment of your birth. The need that I always have, to do good wherever I go, gave me the idea of adopting you as my godson and of endowing you with gentleness and kindness, which in my eyes were the greatest gifts I could offer you.

"Having kissed you and brushed you lightly with my wing as I passed, I continued on my way, because I was on a mission to the queen of the fairies; but my first concern, when I stood before her, was to ask her for permission to make you happy. At first she agreed, but shortly afterward the king of the bumblebees arrived and grew angry with her and with me, and made many threats — shouting that your land had been promised to him and that no one but he had any rights or authority over even the lowliest of its inhabitants.

"For you must know that, at the time, the king of the bumblebees, who had already ruled over your land once before, when he had horribly ravaged and mistreated it, was suffering a dreadful punishment as a result of his evil actions. He had been turned into a common bumblebee, condemned to crawling, hiding himself away, and buzzing around an old oak tree in the forest which he had originally planted with his own hands when he was master and tyrant of the country.

"The king of the bumblebees had been thus transformed for three hundred and eighty-eight years when you came into the world.

"He reminded the queen that she herself has pronounced that his punishment would come to an end in the four hundredth year and that he would then be at liberty to rule over your land once more. 'Consequently,' he said, 'Gentle Jack belongs to me, and the meadowsweet has no right to take him away from me and to fill him with virtue.'

"The queen of the fairies considered for a long time and then gave this decision: 'My daughter, the meadowsweet, has endowed this human child with gentleness and kindness, and no one can destroy a fairy gift pronounced over a cradle. Jack will therefore be gentle and good, but it is true that Jack belongs to you. You will only be freed from your punishment by his hand. The day he says to you, "Fly away and be happy," you will cease to be a common bumblebee. You will be able to leave your old oak tree and reign over the land again. But remember to make Jack very happy, because the day he wishes to leave you, I will allow his godmother to protect him from you.'

"I returned to my island," the queen went on, "and the king of the bumblebees returned to his old oak tree, where twelve years

later to the day, your kindness led you to speak those fateful
words, 'Fly away and be happy.'

"Immediately, the evil insect that had stung you became the
king of the bumblebees once again and took the name of Lord
Bumblebee.

"Jack, you have seen what this evil genius has done. He has
seduced and corrupted the people of your country with his
wealth. He has increased his power by marrying the princess of
the honeybees, who is, in reality, the princess of the hoarders.

"The spirit of greed and theft has stifled the spirit of kindness
and generosity in every heart and has driven into oblivion the
great knowledge which you alone, of all who were born on this
unhappy earth, now possess."

"My dear godmother," said Jack, "I have learned only one
thing, and that was on your island: How to love with all my heart
and to know the joy of being loved — a joy which I had always
dreamed about and had never known before."

"Well," replied the queen, "can you think of anything more
beautiful and essential to learn? You know something that the
people of your country do not."

"So," said Jack, who was beginning to see into his own heart
and to realize that he wasn't so stupid after all, "is it the
knowledge you've given me that will cure the people of my
country of all their wickedness and their sufferings?"

"Of course," replied the queen. "But what does it matter to
you, my dear child? You have nothing more to fear from evil
men; here you are protected from the wrath of the king of the
bumblebees. You will be immortal for as long as you remain on
my island. No sadness will touch you, your days will pass in
centuries of joyful festivities. Come, let us return to the dancing."

Jack looked deep into his heart before replying, and suddenly he threw his arms around his godmother's neck and said, "Smile on me, dear godmother, so that I may not die of grief when I leave you — because leave you I must. No matter that I have neither parents nor friends left in my homeland, I feel that I am the child of that country and must serve it. Since I am the possessor of the most beautiful secret in the world, I must share it with those poor people who hate each other and who are to be pitied. No matter, also, that I'm as happy as the good spirits, thanks to your kindness. I am, nonetheless, a mere mortal, and I want to share my knowledge with other mortals. You have taught me how to love. Well, I feel that I love those evil, mad people who will probably hate me, and I ask you to lead me back among them."

The queen kissed Jack, but she couldn't smile however hard she tried. "Go, my son," she said. "My heart is breaking at leaving you, but I love you all the more because you have understood your duty and because the knowledge I have given you has borne fruit in your soul. I will give you neither a lucky charm nor a magic wand to protect you against the wiles of the evil bumblebees, because it is written in the book of destiny that any mortal who dedicates himself to doing good must risk everything, including life itself. However, I want to help you make the people of your country kinder, so I will allow you to pick from my meadows as many flowers as you wish, and every time a mortal breathes in the scent of even one of these, he will become gentler and more kind. You must then have the wit to take advantage of this. I will not disguise from you that it will be a terrible and dangerous struggle."

Jack picked bunches of flowers and herbs, crying bitterly.

At last he walked down to the shore, where his godmother was waiting for him. In her hand she held a rose from which she plucked a petal and dropped it into the water, saying to Jack, "Here is your ship. May it carry you safely."

She kissed him tenderly and Jack jumped onto the rose petal. In a short time he reached his homeland.

Scarcely had he landed than a crowd of sailors came running, surprised to see a child sailing on a rose petal.

"Well, here's a new invention!" exclaimed the sailors. "How much do you want for it, boy?"

"If my ship pleases you," replied Jack, "take it."

No sooner had he said this than the sailors fell on the boat like madmen, throwing punches at each other, tearing handfuls of hair out of each other's heads, and hurling themselves into the sea in their furious struggle for its possession. But, as the boat was a rose petal from the enchanted island, they had scarcely touched it than its magic power took effect. They were calmed by its sweet perfume and agreed to share the boat and to exhibit it as a curiosity for their mutual profit.

A little later in the day, when the news of Jack's arrival had spread, a crowd assembled and began to shout that the child should be seized, shut up in a cage, and exhibited throughout the country for money.

Whereupon Jack walked into the midst of the crowd, holding his bunch of magic flowers and herbs in front of him and pushing it hastily under the nose of anybody who tried to grab hold of him. No sooner had he done this to some hundred people in the crowd than they surrounded him to protect him from the others. And, little by little, because the flowers from the enchanted island

never withered and they spread a perfume which not even the breath of a hundred thousand people could have exhausted, the whole population of that place was miraculously calmed.

Jack spoke of his island, which anyone could visit providing he was a good person and capable of feeling love. He told them about the happiness that was to be experienced there, the beauty, the tranquillity, the freedom, and the goodness of the inhabitants. And he taught them the lesson that he himself had learned there — the art of loving and being loved.

At last the king of the bumblebees heard of Jack's arrival and the miracles he was performing.

He sent ambassadors to invite Jack to his court.

Jack accepted despite the pleadings of his new friends, who feared the king's evil plans. But Jack wanted to share his treasure with the people of the capital, and he said to himself, "So long as I do good, what does it matter if evil befalls me?"

He was received very warmly by the king, who pretended not to recognize him, and carrying cunning to the extreme, invited him into his private apartment and said to him, "I am told, my dear Jack, that you carry a bunch of flowers which is a sovereign remedy for all ills. Since I have a terrible headache, I would be grateful if you would allow me to smell it."

Jack's only answer was to bring out his precious flowers, which were as fresh as the day he had picked them. He held them before the king, who immediately thrust his poisoned sting into the heart of the loveliest of the roses. A piercing cry and a huge tear burst from the rose, and Jack, stricken with horror and despair, let drop the whole bunch.

The king of the bumblebees seized it, tore it apart, and trampled it beneath his feet, saying to Jack, "There, my sweet child, that's what I think of your lucky charm. Now let us see which of us is the more powerful."

He called his guards, and as Jack no longer had his magic flowers, the boy was seized, bound hand and foot, and thrown into a dark dungeon.

There he was left without food or water. He was fettered with such heavy chains that he couldn't move, and though he never once complained, his jailers heaped coarse insults and hard blows on him.

One night as Jack lay sleepless on the hard ground, he saw something moving in the faint light of a moonbeam and recognized his beloved godmother in the guise of the blue dragonfly.

"Jack," she said to him, "you must be prepared for the worst. The queen of the fairies has at last empowered me to defeat the king of the bumblebees and drive him from the country — but it is on so terrible a condition that I can scarcely tell you what it is."

"Speak, dear godmother," cried Jack. "To secure you the victory and save this unhappy country, I would be prepared to undergo the worst suffering imaginable."

"And if it means death?" asked the meadowsweet in a sad voice.

"If it means death," replied Jack, "may the will of the heavenly powers be done! So long as you remember me with affection, my dear godmother, and if on the Island of Flowers the inhabitants sometimes sing a verse or two in memory of me, I will be content."

"Well, then," said the fairy, "prepare to die, Jack, for tomorrow a new and terrible war will break out, and you will be one of the first victims. Do you feel brave enough?"

"Yes, godmother dear," said Jack.

The fairy kissed him and vanished.

Then Jack, to combat the terror of his approaching death, sang from the depths of his dungeon in a sweet and moving voice, the lovely songs he had learned on the Island of Flowers. The lizards, salamanders, spiders and rats, who were his companions, were so moved by this that they came and sat round Jack and sang his song of death in their turn, each in its own language, while they wept and beat their heads against the walls in grief.

As day dawned, the sound of funeral bells could be heard, followed by a dreadful uproar. Shouts, laughter, curses, and then trumpets, drums, gunfire — as if all hell had been let loose.

The great battle had begun.

The meadowsweet appeared in the sky at the head of a vast army of birds which she had brought with her from her island. At first they seemed like a great black cloud and then like a battalion of winged warriors, as they fell upon the kingdom of the hornets and the bumblebees. At the sight of these reinforcements, those inhabitants of the country opposed to the king took up arms. The king's supporters did the same, and the battle lines were drawn up on a vast plain surrounding the palace.

"The danger is too great," said the king of the bumblebees. "Let us leave these miserable mortals to fight among themselves. There are only just enough of us to defend ourselves against the birds which threaten us."

His wife, the princess of the honeybees, then said to him, "Sire, we will never be able to defend ourselves against the birds. They're as quick as we are and they're better armed. They will devour us by the hundreds. Our only hope of deliverance is to bring the boy, Gentle Jack, the beloved godson of the meadowsweet, from his prison and to tie him to a stake on a bonfire of sulphur and tinderwood. Then we will threaten the enemy queen

that we will set it on fire unless she retreats immediately."

"This time, wife, you are right," said the king. And no sooner said than done. Jack was led to a pyre in the middle of the bumblebee army. A most eloquent stag beetle was sent as an emissary to the meadowsweet to warn her of the king's resolve to burn Jack alive if she decided to continue fighting.

When she saw Jack's plight, the meadowsweet felt her heart begin to break and her courage fail her. She would have given the order to retreat, but Jack, understanding what was in the queen's heart, seized the blazing torch from the hands of the executioner, hurled it into the middle of the fire, and throwing himself into the flames, was consumed in less than an instant.

This was the signal for universal fighting. The two sides fell on each other, but when the king's supporters saw that the royal troops weren't backing them up, they lost heart — and with it, the battle.

While this was happening, the army of the bumblebees and the army of the honeybees were fighting the army of the birds. They had all assumed their magic forms once more, and the horrified humans watched a battle the like of which they had never imagined. Insects as big as men fought furiously against birds, the smallest of which was as large as an elephant. The cruel darts of the stinging insects sometimes struck the sensitive flanks of the larks, warblers, and doves; but the agile tits devoured the honeybees by the thousand, the eagles killed hundreds with one stroke of their wings, and the fabled armor bird ran twenty enemies through in a minute.

At last, after an hour of furious fighting, the army of the bumblebees and their allies littered the battlefield. The wounded birds perched on the trees, where the meadowsweet's smile healed

them instantly. Their victorious queen, who had reassumed the form of a woman of the rarest beauty, flew with her retinue over the bonfire on which Jack had died.

"Mortals," she said to the inhabitants of the kingdom, "lay down your arms and cast aside your hatred. Embrace each other, love one another, forgive, and be happy. The queen of the fairies, speaking through me, commands it."

So saying, the meadowsweet smiled, and at once peace was made with grace and sincerity, as if by a congress of kings.

The crowd then turned to face the remains of the bonfire. There on the ashes a beautiful flower called the *Remember Jack* opened its petals. The meadowsweet picked the flower and placed it tenderly at her breast. Then she and her army took the ashes from the bonfire and flew up into the skies.

First published in the United States 1988 by Dial Books
A Division of NAL Penguin Inc.
2 Park Avenue   New York, New York 10016
Published in Austria 1986 as *Die Geschichte vom Guten Fridolin*
by Österreichischer Bundesverlag Wien
Illustrations copyright © 1986 by Verlag J. F. Schreiber Esslingen
German text copyright © 1986 by Österreichischer Bundesverlag Wien
English text copyright © 1988 by Gela Jacobson and
Methuen Children's Books Ltd.
English translation from *L'histoire du véritable Gribouille*
by George Sand and with reference to the German version,
Die Geschichte vom Guten Fridolin, by Maria Luise Völter
All rights reserved
Printed in Spain
First Edition
1 3 5 7 9 10 8 6 4 2

Library of Congress Cataloging in Publication Data

Sand, George, 1804–1876.
The mysterious tale of Gentle Jack and Lord Bumblebee.

Translation of: *Die Geschichte vom Guten Fridolin.*
Summary: Adopted by the evil Lord Bumblebee, Gentle Jack
refuses to learn to be as wicked as the lord and his followers and
escapes to an island where only goodness is known.
[1. Fairy tales.] I. Spirin, Gennady, ill.
II. Title.
PZ8.S2495My 1988   [Fic]   87-30490
ISBN 0-8037-0538-7